THE ADVENTURES OF PEEK-A-BOO AND PRINCESS CHEYENNE

SHANI SIMMONS

FriesenPress

One Printers Way
Altona, MB R0G 0B0,
Canada

www.friesenpress.com

Copyright © 2021 by Shani Simmons
First Edition — 2021

Forward and poem by Jack Crimmins

Illustrator Muhammad Rizwan Tufail

ISBN
978-1-03-911794-5 (Hardcover)
978-1-03-911793-8 (Paperback)
978-1-03-911795-2 (eBook)

1. JUVENILE FICTION, ANIMALS, CATS

Distributed to the trade by The Ingram Book Company

DEDICATION

There are many people and animals to whom I am grateful. First, Peek-A-Boo and Princess Cheyenne, who were our family's pets; without them, **there would be no story**. Thank you to my family and loving husband, who kept asking, "When are you going to finally finish the book?" To the many friends I tortured by reading the manuscript over and over out loud, and their honest but never brutal critiques.

To Rita, who believed and gave me my start. To Hans, who was so enthusiastic, I felt guilty not finishing, and his three young daughters (who are no longer young), who gave me my very first written review, which was so positive . . . Thank you to Danika, Mikaela, and Segan.

Finally, I want to dedicate this book to my brother, Lee, who died way too young.

FOREWORD

"Shani Simmons' new book, *Peek-A-Boo and Princess Cheyenne*, is cute, fun, a fabulous cats' tale (pun intended) and a teaching story. Touching and precious, this is an adventure that tells of a pampered cat and a stray feral cat who become central to the kind and loving family that adopts them.

Take time to savor this magical journey of a book. This is a heartwarming story, a story for young children, for cat lovers of all ages, and a good way to get to know a couple of cool cats, as well."

~Jack Crimmins, author of the poetry books
Kit Fox Blues, Dancing in the Sun Room,
and *The Rust Life*

DREAMING

Days move slow

in the magic forest.

The winds are here,

dancing in the tall trees.

The cats are nearby,

hidden sometimes,

teaching us about joy.

Everywhere we go

we are dreaming awake.

~Jack Crimmins © 2021

THE ADVENTURES OF PEEK-A-BOO AND PRINCESS CHEYENNE

CHAPTER 1

PEEK-A-BOO'S STORY

Peek-A-Boo's life was harsh. She was unloved. She was born in a field near a barn by an old farmhouse. Her parents were wild cats that no one ever owned. She had many brothers and sisters and was the largest kitten of her family. She knew her momma, but not her dad; he ran away after she was born.

Peek's fur was shaggy and often unkempt as a kitten. It was long in some places and scruffy and short in others. Her coat had lots of different colors. It was black and orange and brown and white, and her little paws looked as if she were wearing white socks.

Because she was a wild cat, Peek had no loving or cuddling from people. In fact, she had no contact with people at all. She neither feared humans nor liked them. She simply had no opinion. As Peek got a bit older, she became more curious about the farmhouse where humans lived, so she decided to wander close to the house. The farmer's wife often swatted at her with the broom yelling, "Shoo away, kitty! I don't want any wild cats 'round here." Still, sometimes Peek's curiosity would get the best of her, especially when the farmer's wife was baking meat pies.

One day, when the farmer's wife accidentally left the front door open, Peek-A-Boo (after carefully looking around) tiptoed into the house. The farmer's wife spotted Peek-A-Boo and let out a shriek.

"What are you doing in my house? Get out, you mangy cat, get out!" Grabbing her broom, she chased the little kitten all around the house, yelling as she ran. "Shoo, git, shoo shoo, git outta here!" she screamed.

Peek-A-Boo was terrified. Her fur puffed straight out. Suddenly, she looked around and spotted the front door still open. Just as she headed through the door, it closed with a loud BANG, catching the tip of her tail inside the door.

"Yaow Yaow Yaow, it hurts!" screamed Peek. She ran as fast as she could into the field, screeching all the while. "Meow, meow meow!" she cried, all the way back to the barn.

All alone with no one to comfort her, Peek limped to her bed in the hay and lay down quietly. Poor Peek mewed softly, licking the tip of her tail repeatedly trying to help it heal. In time, Peek-A-Boo's tail did heal, but the very tip of her tail was now crooked. It wasn't something you could see easily, but she knew it was there, and it reminded her how dangerous people could be. Peek-A-Boo never approached the farmhouse again.

As Peek got older, she became a great hunter. She could catch the fastest field mouse and the largest barn rat even in the more difficult snowy cold of winter. She grew big, with long legs and a bushy tail. She was quite beautiful. Her fur was silky and shiny, and her coat was thick and full. Not ever having seen herself in a mirror, Peek had no idea how magnificent she had grown. She had a black button nose, and her big round eyes were golden with little, green-colored flecks in them. She had long whiskers and a slash of orange fur that ran diagonally from her forehead and across her nose to her chin, making her look like a very fierce cat.

Life was difficult as she got older. She wasn't often happy, and since she wasn't happy, she didn't purr. Winters were the hardest time of the year. When it was snowy and cold, except when she was hunting, she would have to stay curled up in the hay for warmth, and the snow made it harder to scout for food. Mostly, life was lonely for Peek.

One afternoon, in the beginning of the spring thaw, while walking in the field, the farmer's wife saw Peek-A-Boo stalking a field mouse. She went home and waited for her husband to come in from working in the back fields. "Avery, I saw the biggest most beautiful cat I've even seen." She didn't realize Peek was the same cat she shooed out of the house when Peek was a kitten. She continued, "Maybe we oughtta trap her and bring her here to be a mouser for the house. I'll never have to worry about having mice again with that cat living here," she said excitedly.

"Well, just as long as you know that cat is a wild cat, good for mousin' but not the friendly type," said the farmer. They plotted and planned how they would catch this big, beautiful cat. "I know just how to catch her, too," said the farmer.

The next day, the farmer went out into the field closest to the house where his wife had seen Peek-A-Boo hunting the day before. He placed a wooden crate on its side with a stick holding one side of the crate up, and a long, long, long string attached to the stick. Inside the crate, he put a small bowl of milk and some cooked hamburger that was left over from last night's dinner. He then took the string and walked far away so that Peek-A-Boo could neither see nor smell him. Cats have great eyesight and can smell and see things people cannot!

The farmer squatted way down flat on his belly in the field and waited. He waited and waited and waited, and just when he was about to give up waiting, he spotted a cat that looked like the one his wife had described, creeping toward the box. Peek's curiosity about the smells coming from the box, and her hunger, drove her closer and closer to it.

The hamburger and milk were new smells, and the aroma smelled wonderful. *Wow, what is that?* thought Peek. She couldn't resist any longer. She hunched down low to the ground and slowly crept toward the box. Peek looked left and she looked right. She looked in front and she looked behind. As far as Peek could see, there was no one near the box.

She approached the hamburger and milk and began to eat and drink. "Yum, yum, this is so good!" She growled as she ate. Because it tasted so wonderful, she wasn't as cautious as she should have been. BANG!!! The crate came down on her with a loud crash.

Peek-A-Boo panicked. "MEOW, YAW, MEOW!" she screamed as loud as she could. She banged against the crate with her body. She pushed at the sides with all her might and pushed at the top with her head. She scratched and scratched the wooden crate with her claws, but nothing she did could help her escape from the box. "Let me out! LET ME OUT OF HERE! HELLO, HELLO, CAN ANYBODY HEAR ME?" she screamed. Over and over, she yelled and pushed and clawed and screamed, but no one heard her except the farmer. No one helped her.

Eventually, Peek-A-Boo grew very weary. In fact, she was so tired from all the banging, scratching and screaming that all she could do was lie down and rest. The farmer knew that the wild cat would struggle to get out of the box, so he didn't go near the box for an awfully long time. He had on heavy work gloves and a thick, long, brown coat, so that she couldn't scratch him when he took her out from under the box.

Finally, the farmer (who carried a thick canvas bag with tiny breathing holes in it), carefully lifted the lid just a bit and grabbed Peek-A-Boo around the neck. She tried to struggle and scratch him, but his gloves were too thick, and she was very tired. Before she knew what was happening, she was in the canvas bag with the top tied tightly with rope. "Meow, meow, meow!" screeched Peek-A-Boo, trying to wiggle out of the bag, but it was closed too tightly even for her claws.

When the farmer got home that night, he put the bag on the floor. "This cat is full of spit and vinegar," he said to his wife. "Be careful when I open this bag cause she's gonna come out hissin', spittin, n' fightin'." Having said that, he carefully opened the top of the canvas bag and jumped back.

Peek-A-Boo leaped out of the bag. Her fur was standing straight out. Her eyes were wild. She hissed and swatted at the farmer and his wife, ran around the house, up the steps and hid under the first bed she could find. She then stuffed herself tightly into a ball in a corner under the bed and waited.

"Put a saucer of milk down and leave the cat alone. She'll come out when she's hungry enough. There are plenty of mice 'round here for her to catch for her supper," said the farmer.

The farmer and his wife ate their dinner, watched some television, and went to bed. For the next few days, Peek was extremely quiet. She would hide under the bed all during the day, and when it was quiet at night and the people had gone to sleep, she would come out, explore the house, drink the milk left for her, and catch a mouse for her dinner. This became Peek-A-Boo's life for the next few years.

One day, the farmer's wife decided she wanted a pet. "Avery, I want a pet cat. You're gone most of the day and I am alone. I know that this wild cat can never be a pet, so I am going to drive into the city to the pound and see if I can adopt a cat," said the farmer's wife. She was in luck. She adopted a big old black male cat named Francis.

Francis was an incredibly lazy cat, and not used to going outside at all. He had been the companion of an elderly lady, who spoiled him with treats and let him do whatever he wanted. When the lady died, her family didn't want Francis, so they took him to the pound to be adopted. He had never been with other cats and was used to having the whole house to himself, but the pound didn't know that. His schedule was to sleep during the day and roam around the house at night, although that information was also not on his adoption papers.

The farmer's wife, not knowing Francis's history, brought him home that day. He liked her from the very beginning and sat on her lap during their TV time, purring while she petted him. He slept on her lap until the farmer and his wife went to bed. Then Francis decided to explore the house. He was just trotting around the corner from the living room to the kitchen when he came face-to-face with Peek-A-Boo, who was out looking for mice.

"Who are you? What are you doing in my house? Get out!" he caterwauled. He had a very deep, loud voice and huge black piercing eyes.

Peek wasn't used to seeing other cats, let alone one as big as Francis. "Excuse me," she meowed very politely, "but I live here."

"Not if I can help it," growled the big black cat. With that, Francis started to chase Peek around the house, swatting at her with his long, dangerous claws. They ran and fought and growled, making a terrible noise. Suddenly Peek got tangled up in a large mound of electrical cords, including the cord to an awfully expensive family lamp. Before she knew what was happening, Francis, with an evil glint in his eyes and a smirk on his lips, pushed over the lamp. It fell to the floor with a loud CRASH.

"That will teach you. I'm gonna tell the farmer you broke the lamp," said Francis. Then Francis ran out of the room, up the steps, and into the bedroom where the farmer and his wife had been sleeping. The farmer had already jumped out of bed from the loud noise.

"Meow, meow, wake up and see what that nasty cat downstairs has done," Francis tattled to the farmer.

When the farmer got downstairs, Peek was still struggling to get out of the bunch of cords, and was very, very afraid. The farmer was sure that Peek-A-Boo had broken the lamp and yelled at her while trying to untangle the cords. "Dratted cat, stay still, darn you! Darn cat! I should have known better than to let you into my house. You're nothin' but trouble!"

As he touched Peek, she panicked, scratched his arm and bit his hand. She didn't mean to hurt him, but she was frightened. When she got loose, she ran as fast as she could up the steps and under the bed in the guest room. She could hear the farmer still yelling. "I'm gonna kill that that cat when I get a hold of her!" Peek shook with fear. She knew she was in trouble, but she just didn't understand what was happening or why.

The next day the farmer put on his heavy coat and gloves, picked up the canvas bag, marched into the guest room and closed the door. He then tilted the bed to get Peek out from under it. There was no other place to hide.

"You're going to the pound, you dang cat. I don't want a cat 'round here that's gonna hurt somebody." He chased Peek round and round the room until he caught her. The next thing she knew, she was in the bag and being taken away.

When the bag was opened again, Peek's surroundings were completely different. Here was a cold steel cage with not much in it except a bowl of water, a box with some gravel-like stuff in it, and a small blanket to lie on. She was afraid of people now, so she hid in the corner of the cage and hissed when anyone came near. When she was finally left alone, she fell asleep.

CHAPTER 2

CHEYENNE'S STORY

Cheyenne was the most beautiful kitten in the world. She had long silky fur that was pure white. Her eyes were the color of a copper pot and seemed almost too big for her little face. No one before or since had ever seen eyes like hers, and everyone who saw her instantly fell in love with her. Cheyenne's nose was tiny and flat against her face, which didn't allow her to smell very well. People could hear her smelling things by the sound she made with her nose. "SSSSSnnnniiiiiiffff, SSSSSnnnniiiiiiffff" she would sniff loudly.

Her mother and father were famous Persian show cats whose owner took them all around the country, winning many ribbons and much money. *I know I will win contests just like my parents*, thought Cheyenne. *That is why I get bathed with perfumes, have bows in my fur, and even have a collar with fancy stones on it! I am the most beautiful kitten ever,* she thought.

Unfortunately, as Cheyenne grew older, her tear ducts (where tears come out) didn't close properly. She always looked as if she was crying with big brown streaks under her eyes.

"What are we going to do now? I have spent a great deal of time on Cheyenne to be a show cat, and the vet says her eye drip will never go away!" Mrs. Andrews said as she sat at the kitchen table, crying. She had expected her little cat would win many cat shows.

After a few minutes, she stopped crying, blew her nose, stood up, and said, "I was talking to Mrs. Smith down the street. I know their boys would love to have a kitten. All right, I have decided, I will give her to them, but I am disappointed. I thought she was going to be a champion." Soon, Mrs. Andrews called the Smith family, and Cheyenne had a new home.

In the beginning, the Smith boys carried Cheyenne everywhere like she was a baby. "She is sooooo cute and fluffy. I think she's a princess!" said the youngest son, and over time, the name stuck. Her new name was Princess Cheyenne.

I am the most beautiful, most loved kitty in the whole wide world, Cheyenne thought as she looked in the mirror. *I think I will let everyone know how happy I am, purrrrrr purrrrrr purrrr.*

Since she was happy most of the time, she purred most of the time. Soon, she began to kitty-talk. "Meow, meow, bbbbbrrrrra, bbbbrrrraaa," she would say while rubbing her head against their legs. "Meow, meow, pick me up and give me some loving!" she would say. Now, Cheyenne could have easily jumped into her owners' laps, but she was lazy. "Why should I jump when I know they will pick me up and cuddle me?" Cheyenne said. And she was right. The more she talked, the more people responded to her, so the more she talked.

Her life was easy and simple. She ate, slept, played, and was loved. It was the perfect life.

In the springtime, Princess Cheyenne ate her breakfast of warm milk and cooked chicken, and then went out into the garden to chase bugs and butterflies. The butterflies were her friends . . . the bugs, not so much. She would swat the bugs with her paw and sometimes try to eat them.

"Yuck, you taste terrible," said the kitten.

"Well then, don't bug us!" yelled the bugs running away toward the grass.

"Oh well, I'm tired. I think I will stretch out and take a nap in the sun. I love the spring; it is my favorite time of the year," said the princess to no one in particular, and then she promptly fell asleep.

In the fall, she would follow the boys outside, jumping in and out of the piles of leaves they raked, scattering them everywhere until the boys yelled for her to get away.

"Come on Princess Cheyenne, you're making a big mess, and I just raked there!" they would shout.

She played until she was tired and then went in the house and curled up in the window, watching them work until she fell asleep. Her last thought was, *I think my favorite time of the year is fall.*

Her family lived where it snowed. The snow was the same color as Cheyenne; pure white, which helped her disappear when she went outside. She was never cold because her coat was now long and thick. Chy Chy, (the nickname the boys had given her), would hide in the deep snow, wait for one of the boys to walk past, and then pounce on their boots.

"Here, Chy Chy, catch this!" said the youngest son, throwing snowballs. They played and played until their mother called them in.

"Boys, Chy Chy, time to get out of the snow!" yelled their mother. "You two go upstairs and change into dry clothes. Cheyenne, come let me dry you off, and I'll give you a saucer of warm milk and cooked chicken." The big soft towel felt wonderful, and the warm chicken tasted great.

You know, she thought, *Winter is my favorite time of the year.*

The only part of her life she didn't like was her bath time. Mrs. Smith would take Cheyenne to a cat groomer to be bathed and brushed. Cheyenne hated the water, mostly because of the way it made her look when she was wet: scrawny, with soggy fur. When it was time for the family to take her to the groomer, Cheyenne would run and hide under the sofa.

"No, no I don't want to go," she yelled. She would meow and run from one room to the other until someone caught her and placed her in the carrier.

All the way to the groomer she would complain loudly, "Pleeeezzzz don't take me there . . . pleeeezzzz!" she would cry over and over. She complained the whole time she was being bathed.

"It's okay, Chy Chy, you're going to be beautiful when we're finished, and you'll get a lovely ribbon," said the groomer. The groomer always tied a brightly colored bow on Cheyenne's fur.

Cheyenne would prance back and forth, looking in the mirror. She was even more beautiful than before. The streaks under her eyes were temporarily gone, and her long white fur was silky and flowing. The family would *oooohhhh* and *aaahhhh* while hugging her, making her hatred of bath time forgotten . . . until the next time.

There were other pets in the Smith household, although if you asked Cheyenne's opinion, she was the most important pet in the family. There was an old gray cat named Gray Girl, and a huge female dog named Trinket. Gray Girl liked Cheyenne from the moment the princess arrived as a kitten. The old gray cat had never had kittens of her own, and this gave her the chance to be a mama cat. Cheyenne liked old Gray Girl and often curled up with her to sleep.

The big dog loved both cats and wanted to play with them constantly, but the old cat had no patience for the dog and would skulk away, grumbling to herself.

"You are a dog! You are not supposed to like cats! *Hisssss hissssss*, go away Trinket, I have no energy for your nonsense."

"I'll play with you," said the princess as she pounced on Trinket's back from the dining room chair. They would play for hours until the older dog became tired and went off to the sofa to sleep.

"No more," she growled at the kitten, "I'm tired." But before Trinket put her head down to sleep, her enormous tongue would lick the little princess's face. The three pets lived happily together for several years.

Then life changed. Trinket grew old. She couldn't move around well anymore and stopped playing with Cheyenne.

"What is the matter with you, Trinket? Why don't you run and play with me anymore?"

"Cheyenne, stop tapping me on my nose, I am tired," said the old dog.

"Come on Trinket, let's play. I'll jump on the chair and then jump on your back," Cheyenne said jumping all around the dog.

"No, little one, not today. Maybe I'll feel better tomorrow," said Trinket.

Often, Trinket would lie on the sofa for days at a time. On these days, Chy Chy would lie beside the big dog and try to cheer her up.

Then one day, Trinket didn't move off the sofa at all. The family knew Trinket had died. Mr. Smith and the two boys buried Trinket in the backyard by the garden where they had played together, while Mom, Cheyenne, and Gray Girl stood close together and watched. It was a sad day for everyone.

"I am sad. I miss Trinket. Can I sleep with you tonight, Gray Girl?" asked Cheyenne.

"I miss Trinket too, little one," said the old grey cat while snuggling with the little, white princess as they fell asleep.

Not too long after that, Gray Girl, who had grown quite old herself, passed away in her sleep, and the family buried her next to Trinket in the garden.

"I don't have anyone I can play with now. Please play with me," Cheyenne would say to the Smith boys, but the boys were getting a bit older, each having school-work and after-school activities, so they played with her less and less.

One day, Mr. Smith came home from work extremely excited. "I got a promotion at work, so we can buy that larger house we liked!" exclaimed Mr. Smith with glee. Everybody was excited . . . except Cheyenne.

"I don't know what is going on around here, but I don't think I like it," said the princess. There was much hustle and bustle as boxes were filled and the family began packing up their things getting ready for their move. At first, it seemed fun jumping in and out of empty boxes.

"Cheyenne, get out of that box. I am trying to pack!" yelled the older son.

"MEOW! I don't like this change. Pay more attention to me!" she yelled. At nighttime, she would roam from room to room and box to box, yelling her dissatisfaction. "Hey, wake up everyone, pay attention to me. Everybody WAKE UP! I am lonely and bored," she screamed with her loudest voice.

The family started picking her up and petting her just to keep her quiet and happy.

"Ah ha," she purred loudly. "I am the princess, and there is no one else around here to get all the attention and love now but me."

After the chaos of the move, everyone was settling into their new home. The family then focused much of their time and attention on Cheyenne again. She became very spoiled and self-centered. It remained that way until her eighth birthday.

CHAPTER 3

THE ADOPTION

Peek-A-boo was awakened by the sound of voices and someone opening the cage door. She quickly backed into a corner and started hissing and swatting at the lady that was coming to get her.

"I don't know if this one will ever be able to be adopted. She seems wild and too afraid of people for a family to take her home," the lady said. "We'll just have to see how she does after we spay her and give her shots."

The lady grabbed Peek and quickly and carefully wrapped her tightly in a towel so she wouldn't be bitten. Peek-A-Boo noticed the lady wasn't hurting her, and the lady's voice was incredibly soft. After everything she had been through, this gentleness was both new and welcome. Also, Peek-A-Boo had never been held before. It was a different kind of experience. It felt strange, awkward, and yet good, even though she was still afraid.

She was carried into a room that was very cold and when she awoke, she was back in her cage. She noticed some of her fur was gone and just below her tummy area hurt a little. There were tiny little stitches there. She licked and licked at the stitches, trying to heal them.

The lady came back and softly spoke to her. "Hello kitty cat, how are you feeling today?" She opened the cage and tried petting Peek-A-Boo's head and ears, but Peek jerked her head away, hissing (but only slightly). Then the lady cautiously and gently moved her to check the stitches. Peek hissed at the lady, but not very convincingly. She was still much too weak to fight.

"Well, now, it looks like everything is healing nicely, so I am going to give you something to eat," she said. Peek gratefully accepted the soft food and ate slowly, still cautious and a wee bit drowsy.

Over time, the stitches dissolved, and she felt much better. The lady came regularly, petted Peek-A-Boo, and often changed her litter box. Peek, who had always gone to the bathroom out in the field, wasn't sure what the box was for but used it anyway. The lady also came twice a day to give Peek fresh food and water, all the while speaking to her in a quiet voice.

"Well, it seems you're not such a tough gal after all. Maybe we will be able to adopt you out to a nice family. You're a beautiful lady, you know that don't you?"

Much to Peek-A-Boo's surprise, she began to look forward to the lady's visits.

One day, when the lady was holding Peek-A-Boo, something strange started to happen. A place deep down in her body started to vibrate. The more the lady petted her, the faster the vibration. She was purring. *PPPPPUURRRRRRRRRRRR   PPPPUURRRRRRRRRRR,* came from her throat. The purr was strong and loud. It surprised both Peek-A-Boo and the lady.

"Wow, you can purr after all. I think you are almost ready for people to see you now, and maybe I can adopt you out to a nice family," said the lady.

In the next few weeks, lots of people came and went, peering into Peek's cage and reading the note the pound had written about her. **Mixed breed Persian cat with**

no name, the note said. **Purrs when you scratch her ears and belly. Age: about five years old. Weight: twelve pounds. Gets along with other cats**. Many people looked at Peek, but usually they thought she was too big, too old, not a kitten, or not friendly enough for most people. Peek wasn't mean anymore; she didn't hiss or spit, as that just wasn't her nature, but she was still shy and cautious. She remembered that some humans were not particularly kind.

One day, a man, woman, and two boys came to the pound looking for a large cat that wasn't a kitten. A cat that could get along with the cat they already had at home. They wanted a cat that needed lots of love and attention. The pound lady quickly thought about Peek-A-Boo and took the family to see her. The man looked at lots of other cats, but the lady instantly fell in love with Peek-A-Boo. She put her finger through the wires of the cage and let Peek smell her finger.

Peek rubbed her head and ears against the lady's finger. The cat seemed friendly enough. The lady asked to see Peek-A-Boo in the large show room to see how friendly she was. They waited and waited and finally the pound lady came in holding Peek-A-Boo. She put her on the floor and let her walk around. Peek smelled everything. She smelled the floor, she smelled the walls, she smelled the feet of the chairs, and she cautiously smelled the hands of the people. The man petted Peek and spoke to her in a sweet, loving tone.

"Hello, pretty girl. You are a big beauty, aren't you? Would you like to come home with us?" asked the man.

Peek didn't know why, but she instantly liked and trusted this man. Maybe it was the soft sing-song tone of his voice. She slowly flopped down on her back for the man to scratch her belly. It felt so good, and he was so gentle that she started to purr very loudly. One by one, the lady and two boys petted her and scratched her belly.

"What do you think?" the man said. "I really like this one."

The boys and lady quickly agreed, so they signed the papers, paid the money for the care of the cat, and soon after, Peek-A-Boo was on her way to her new home and a new adventure.

CHAPTER 4

MEETING A PRINCESS

Peek-A-Boo was put into a case with a soft furry bottom for her to curl up in, and windows to look out of to see where she was going. The case felt safe and warm. A short time later, she was brought inside a large house. The people opened the door to the case to let her out and walked away to give her space to explore her new home.

Peek, still cautious, waited until she didn't see the people around before she crept out. Everything smelled new and different. There were windows that were huge (from the floor to the ceiling), and the polished wooden floors were very slippery. Peek saw stairs and knew there would be beds to hide under, so up the steps she ran and hid under the nearest bed.

Mrs. Smith saw her run up the stairs and quickly followed her. "Here kitty, come out," said Mrs. Smith softly, but Peek was still somewhat cautious, so she stayed under the bed. When nighttime came, Peek came out from under the bed to walk around her new house and catch a mouse for supper. After all, that was what Peek was used to doing when she lived in the farmhouse.

"Wow, there are so many windows here. I think I'll try to sit in all of them," she said. So, she sat in one while looking around the room. She then looked around, but could not find a mouse to eat anywhere, and her stomach was growling.

"I'm hungry," she said out loud. Suddenly, she heard a noise above her head. She looked up and on the top of the counter she saw a cat with the biggest eyes she had ever seen, looking at her from above. "Hello there, who are you?" Cheyenne asked. Before the cat could say another word, Peek remembered her experience with Francis at the farmhouse and ran as fast as she could back up the steps and under the bed.

The next day, the people tried to talk Peek out from her hiding place, but she still wouldn't come out, so they just left her alone. At night, Peek came out again, looking for mice. She was very, very hungry and needed something to eat and drink. She went downstairs and looked everywhere, under the furniture, in the corners, and even on the countertops. She opened lower cabinet doors with her claws, but there was not a mouse to be found anywhere.

Peek-A-Boo was getting desperate. She looked up again on the countertop and saw the fluffy white cat with the big eyes looking at her.

"You weren't nice to me last night. I said hello to you, and you ran away. That's impolite. Don't you have any manners?" asked the princess. The white cat then licked her paw and cleaned her eyes. "I am the Princess Cheyenne, and you will address me as such," she meowed. "Just who are you?" asked the princess.

Peek thought a minute, realizing that this cat was a much smaller cat, not like Francis at all. "I'm sorry, I do have manners, you just startled me. I'm a cat," said Peek.

"Well, of course you are a cat, silly. So, am I, but what is your name?" Cheyenne asked.

Peek-A-Boo thought for some moments, and then said, "I don't think I have a name. How did you get a name?" asked Peek.

"My owners gave me my name," the princess said. "I suppose they will give you one too. Everything that's important around here has a name. This is my palace, and you must ask me for permission before doing anything. I am royalty," exclaimed the princess.

Peek-A-Boo didn't know what royalty meant but thought better of saying so to this new cat. Anyway, she was too hungry to continue this conversation. She had to find a mouse. "Do you know where I can find a mouse for dinner?" she asked.

The princess laughed so hard she almost fell off the counter. Wiping tears from her eyes, she said, "A mouse? There are no mice here in my palace!"

"Well, what do you eat then? I am starving!" exclaimed Peek-A-Boo.

Cheyenne jumped down from the countertop and pranced across the floor, her long, bushy, white tail standing high above her back. She slowly came to two bowls sitting off in a corner of the kitchen floor and bent her head down to drink daintily from her water bowl. "Here is my food and water. You can eat a bit if you must," she said. Chy Chy then jumped into the kitchen window, still watching this strange cat.

Peek walked over to the two bowls and smelled what was in them. She quickly drank some water. She knew what that was, but the stuff in the other bowl was new to her. It wasn't a mouse, and it wasn't like the food at the pound, either. She sniffed it and batted it with her paw. Then she carefully ate what had stuck to her claws. It tasted different, and good! She ate heartily and when she could eat no more, she looked around and saw the white cat still watching her.

"What kind of food was that?" she asked, cleaning her face with her paw.

"Don't you know anything? It is gourmet cat food," said Princess Cheyenne. "I only eat the best. Sometimes it is lamb, sometimes beef or chicken, and some-times fish."

"How do they put a sheep or a cow or chicken into that small bag?" asked Peek. Coming from a farm, she knew about real animals, but not store-bought cat food.

"Boy, you are dumb!" said Cheyenne, never considering she might be hurting the new cat's feelings. "Cat food comes in different flavors from the grocery store. Sometimes it's wet and sometimes it's dry. I get different ones each week."

At this point, Cheyenne was getting bored with the conversation. She bored easily if the topic of conversation wasn't about her. She pranced over to the sofa in the living room, jumped on a blanket, and pretended to sleep.

Now, Peek needed to go to the bathroom. "Excuse me, Cheyenne, but can you show me where your dirt pit is, or the cat box, so I can go to the bathroom?"

Cheyenne lazily stretched, opened one eye, and looked down at Peek-A-Boo. "That's *Princess* Cheyenne to you, and I go to the bathroom in a box in that room over there. I don't know what a dirt pit is, but you can't use my box; it's mine."

By now, Peek had to go to the bathroom badly. She thought that the princess was being mean to her, but at least they weren't fighting like her experience with Francis. She trotted to the other room, inspected the box for a moment or two, climbed in, and went. When she was finished, she went back into the other room to talk to Princess Cheyenne, but noticed she was sleeping. Peek then went upstairs and back under the bed where she felt safe. At least now her belly was full, and she knew where to get food and water when she needed it.

Whenever the people would come into the room, she would back herself into the corner under the bed and watch them.

One day, Mrs. Smith was talking to Mr. Smith about the new cat. "I think we should call her Peek-A-boo, since she only comes out at night, or just 'peeks' around the corners when we are awake."

Mr. Smith and the boys agreed that the name was a good one for their new cat, and so Peek-A-Boo was officially named. She continued to live in this same routine for a few months, eating, exploring, and hiding.

"Princess, would you show me around the rest of the house?" asked Peek one day when the family was gone. She finally had the courage to explore her new home.

"I have to sleep during the day while the Smiths are at work and school," said Cheyenne. "I have to get my beauty rest, so I will be beautiful, refreshed, and ready to play when everyone gets home. Look around for yourself," Cheyenne said.

Wow, she is mean, thought Peek-A-Boo.

CHAPTER 5

RACCOON RELATIVES

In the room where Peek was hiding under the bed, there was also a sofa with a fluffy quilt on it, a large desk with a computer, a printer, and a stack of papers. There were many bookshelves with books everywhere, and a big soft chair near the door. This door, which opened to a small balcony, had lots of small square windowpanes, and the room smelled like the man.

Peek could jump on the bed and look outside whenever she wanted. It was warm in the mornings when the sun came in the room, and Peek decided it would be nice to lie on the bed and soak up the sun. She did this for a month before deciding to explore other parts of the house. Usually, she would stay on the bed all day except for going down to eat and drink, and only go under the bed when she heard the people coming home.

After being comfortable in her room, Peek explored the other rooms in the house. She discovered a room that had a big bowl with water in it. The bowl was deep and trying to drink water from it was tricky. Peek practiced and practiced trying to drink water from the bowl and not get her paws wet. Once, she even fell in the bowl, becoming completely soaked! The water was cold, and she had to lick herself to get warm and dry. The room with the bowl was brightly colored and had many mirrors.

One day, Peek jumped up on the counter and peered into the mirror. What she saw was a big colorful cat staring back at her. She had never seen her own reflection before. She hissed and ran into the hallway to get away from the cat.

"Princess Cheyenne, come quick. There's another cat in the house!" yelled Peek.

Cheyenne ran up the steps and went into the bathroom to investigate this new cat. She looked high and low for a new cat but didn't find any. "There is no other cat up here," Chy said to Peek-A-Boo.

"Oh yes there is, and I will prove it to you!" With that, Peek snuck back into the room with mirrors. She jumped on the counter and saw the same big cat staring at her again. Peek hissed again and swatted at the big cat.

Cheyenne shook her head in disbelief. "Don't you know what that is?" asked Cheyenne. "That's a mirror, and it's your own reflection you're seeing. You are seeing yourself! Where have you lived all your life, under a rock, in a barn?" asked the princess.

"As a matter of fact, I was born in a barn," said Peek.

"Well," replied Cheyenne, "I can believe that."

Peek-A-Boo was too busy looking at her own reflection to worry about another insult from Cheyenne. *Wow*, thought Peek-A-Boo, *is that really what I look like? Well, well, I am good looking, and a big cat!* Peek looked at herself for a long time. She pranced to the right and then turned and pranced to the left. She put her nose right up to the mirror and smelled. It didn't smell like her.

Cheyenne watched Peek look at herself and shook her pretty head. *How sad*, she thought, *this cat really thinks she's pretty. Doesn't she know, I am the pretty one?*

"By the way," Cheyenne said as she was leaving the bathroom, "don't drink the water from the big white bowl in here. The humans use it as their 'dirt pit.'" Cheyenne snickered as she left, knowing that Peek had already been drinking out of the bowl.

Peek shook her head, stuck out her tongue, and ran down the steps as fast as she could to drink clean water. She tried not to remember that she not only had drunk from the bowl just a few minutes before, but that she had also fallen in . . .

Thank goodness the princess never saw me do that, or I would never hear the end of it, she thought to herself. Soon after the discovery of the mirror, Peek came downstairs to explore the rest of the house. Since the mirror was exciting, surely there would be other things equally as exciting down there.

The living room was large and had a fireplace that smelled of burnt trees. There were huge windows all around the living room, the sunroom, and the kitchen.

She could watch the birds and squirrels while very much enjoying the sun. She started making a habit of coming downstairs when nobody was home. The sun was warm and toasty, and she loved looking at the trees and small birds.

One day, while Peek was sunning in the living room, she heard Cheyenne talking to someone in the sunroom. She went into the room and saw Cheyenne talking to an animal on the other side of the door.

"Come on out and play," the voice from outside hissed to Cheyenne. "I am your cousin, and I want to play with you." Peek was curious. She wanted to meet Cheyenne's cousin. Little Cheyenne's face was pressed against the windows of the door, trying to decide whether she should push the small cat door open and go outside or not. As Peek headed toward the door, she realized that these cousins weren't cousins at all. They were raccoons!

The king, or head raccoon was trying to convince Cheyenne to come out of the house, since he was too big to fit through her cat door. Peek had seen raccoons kill small cats at the farm and knew that Cheyenne was naïve about wild animals outside of the house. The princess didn't know what raccoons were, or just how vicious they could be.

Just as Chy was about to go through the cat door, Peek-A-Boo jumped on her, knocking her over, and stopping her from going outside. She had fought with raccoons when she lived on the farm. They had sharp claws, sharp teeth, and sometimes carried diseases, and these raccoons were much bigger than Cheyenne.

Cheyenne scampered around the room and jumped on the back of the sofa in the sunroom. Her fur was puffed out and she was truly angry. "What did you do that for? I was just going outside to meet my cousins and play with them!" she shouted.

Peek put her face right up to the door of the sunroom and spoke to the raccoon king. "Don't ever come around here again!" she hissed. "If you do, I will fight you. I know who you are, and I am as big as you," she snarled. She threw her weight against the door, her claws open, scratching at the glass trying to frighten the king. The raccoons chattered amongst themselves, and then suddenly the big one lunged at the door.

Cheyenne was very frightened. She jumped down and hid under the sofa. Peek-A-Boo growled, hissed, swatted with her claws, and threw herself at the small windowpanes in the door, trying to scare them. She really didn't want to go outside to fight them if she didn't have to. The raccoons chattered excitedly again, the big one turning to look at Peek-A-Boo, who hissed and swatted at the door once more. Then after a lot more chatter, the raccoons decided to leave the area; at least for the time being. Slowly, they went away, the biggest of the raccoons glaring at Peek-A-Boo as he waddled away.

Peek turned to look for Princess Cheyenne to scold her. "They are wild animals and dangerous. You are a house cat, and you could have been seriously hurt, or even killed! Don't ever go outside when they are around," she scolded. Peek checked once more to make sure the raccoons had left. Then she went back upstairs, jumping on the bed and washing her face, all the while muttering to herself, "The princess thinks I am a country bumpkin. She doesn't even know that raccoons are dangerous. She is vain and silly . . ."

Then Peek heard a noise at the door of the bedroom and jumped. She was about to dive under the bed when she turned to see Princess Cheyenne at the door.

"Excuse me," said Cheyenne. "May I come in and speak with you for a minute?"

Before Peek could say anything, Cheyenne had jumped on the bed and was walking slowly toward Peek-A-Boo. "I don't know what to say. I guess you saved me from doing a very ummm, ummm . . ." Cheyenne paused, trying to come up with the proper word.

"Stupid," interrupted Peek-A-Boo.

"No, that's not what I was going to say," snapped Cheyenne. "I was going to say, **silly** thing. Anyway, I just came up to say, well, ah, well—" Cheyenne swallowed and stammered. She, the princess, was not used to saying she was sorry to anyone, let alone a farmhouse cat.

Peek-A-Boo was enjoying every moment. She knew that apologizing was not something Her Highness liked to do. "Yes, you were saying?" said Peek with a hint of laughter in her eyes.

"Oh, all right then, I'm sorry I was mean to you . . . and thank you for saving me," Cheyenne said as fast as she could get the words out. "There, I said it!" And with that, Cheyenne jumped down off the bed and pranced downstairs.

The incident was never spoken of again, but something had changed in their relationship. Peek believed it was the beginning of a friendship, never knowing that Cheyenne was vengeful and never to be trusted.

One day, a while after Peek-A-Boo had been living in her new home, she went downstairs to be in the sunroom, just as she usually did, not realizing that the man of the house was still home. She found him napping on the couch in the sunroom. Instead of running away, her curiosity got the best of her, so Peek jumped on the top edge of the couch to see if she could go near him and not be afraid. She carefully walked along the edge of the couch top, never taking her eyes off Mr. Smith as she moved.

Mr. Smith sensed that Peek was on the couch and opened his eyes just a sliver but didn't move a muscle. Peek-A-Boo took a chance and walked up the man's leg, sniffing as she went, and then on to his chest. She peered into his eyes, which were now open, ready at any moment to jump off and run away.

The man spoke softly. "Hello there, Peek-A-Boo. This is certainly a surprise. I'm glad you finally decided to come and visit while I am here." He slowly lifted his hand to pet her. Peek hissed at him, jumped off, and ran upstairs.

Cheyenne, who was watching, just shook her head. **She is certainly missing out on a lot of affection,** thought Cheyenne, **which is great for me, because I will get it all!** With that, the princess jumped on the sofa and curled up in Mr. Smith's lap enjoying the affection that was meant for Peek-A-Boo.

It took almost a year before Peek-A-Boo fully trusted the Smith family enough to let them pet her or pick her up and cuddle her. Even then, it had to be from a high place like the top of the sofa, or a desk, cat tree, or chair, for Peek never learned to trust getting close to people while she was on the floor. Even the Smith boys, whom she learned to love dearly, and who cuddled her often, were only allowed to pet, cuddle, or pick her up after she was off the floor using a chair or steps or table for height.

CHAPTER 6

THE LIE

About three and a half years after Peek-A-Boo arrived at her new home, things changed again. The Smith family was boxing everything up and moving to a smaller place. Cheyenne wasn't disturbed at all about the move. She had done this several times with the family and knew the whole routine. But it was a different story for Peek-A-Boo. She was comfortable living here. She had grown to trust the kindly couple and their sons, and she had created a routine that suited her disposition. She would sun in the morning, eat in the early afternoon, and visit with the family in the evening. She even played with the princess when Cheyenne was in the mood. Now it was all going to change, and this made Peek extremely nervous.

"What if they don't want me? What if they take me back to the pound? What if I haven't been friendly enough or cuddly enough for them?" she asked the princess with panic in her voice. Now, over the last several years, Peek had learned not to trust everything that the princess said to her. Sometimes Cheyenne was jealous. Sometimes, she said things to hurt Peek's feelings. Often, she would try to chase Peek away when the man or woman was giving Peek-A-Boo more attention than Cheyenne.

When something was broken, Cheyenne would drop out of sight so the family would blame Peek-A-Boo. But the family seemed to know better, and Peek rarely got in trouble. Now Peek-A-Boo was so upset about the move, she forgot to not trust Cheyenne's opinion. Cheyenne thought, *this is a great opportunity to get rid of the competition once and for all.*

Certainly not thinking about the consequences of not telling the truth, Cheyenne lied to Peek-A-Boo.

"Well," Cheyenne began, in the softest, sweetest voice ever, "maybe you are right. Maybe you are just not cuddly enough for them. Maybe that is why we are moving, so the family can take you back to the pound." Cheyenne knew it didn't have to make sense because Peek was already so scared. "Perhaps you should leave before they take you away again. Otherwise, you will probably wind up at the pound looking for another family. In a smaller house, there won't be room for two cats," said Cheyenne.

Peek mistakenly thought that Cheyenne was her friend. She was heartbroken but was determined not to go back to the pound. She thought over what Cheyenne had said and knew it would be best for her to leave. Peek-A-Boo said goodbye to the princess, clawed at the back door to slightly open it, and ran out into the unfamiliar world of the countryside.

Cleaning her face and smiling, Cheyenne watched Peek leave, knowing she would now get all the attention she wanted from the family, and certainly not thinking about how the family would feel with Peek gone. In fact, all that she could think about was how much fun it was going to be not having to compete for affection, when all the family got to their new home. Cheyenne was pleased with herself for pulling off the lie. She washed her face, drank some water, and stretched out on the sofa to get some sleep before the family returned from moving more boxes.

CHAPTER 7

CHEEKY & MEGAN

It was a warm day. The sun was shining brightly as Peek-A-Boo wandered around the garden. She had left her home and run away from the people she was convinced would take her back so to the pound. She had been walking for what seemed like hours when she saw a beautiful garden. Peek hadn't seen a garden in years, and it was so nice to walk among the flowers and vegetables. She enjoyed the sun so much; she stretched out between the rows of flowers and began to fall asleep.

Tap, tap, tap . . . something tapped her on the nose. Peek opened one eye and saw she was nose-to-nose with a squirrel.

"Pardon me, but you are sleeping right smack dab in the middle of my garden," said the squirrel, completely unafraid of the cat. "Let me introduce myself," he said. "I am Cheeky, and as I said, you are an intruder in my garden."

Peek opened both eyes, stretched, yawned, and looked at the little squirrel. *Hmmm,* she thought, *this is certainly a different kind of squirrel.* All the squirrels that lived on the farm were gray, with big bushy tails, and they really feared cats. This one was all black with a scraggily black tail that had a tiny white tip on it. Peek also remembered that squirrels were very talkative and talked way too fast. In fact, it was commonly known that squirrels were chatterboxes.

As she was thinking about the farm, she was jolted from her memories by another tap on the nose. This time, it was a good bit harder.

"Are you listening to me?" asked Cheeky. "I would appreciate it if you moved, so I can continue burying my nuts for the winter. I store everything here in my garden, so I know where to find it when I need it. Don't you have a home of your own somewhere? I should think so. You're big and well cared for. I am sure you have a family of your own. I, however, am alone in this world, and take care of myself. Sooo, you will just have to move along now, and leave me to my work. By the way, would you like to know how I got my name? Humans gave it to me because I am very bold and not afraid of them. Are you afraid of humans? Some are really nice, but some you have to watch out for!" chattered Cheeky.

Just as Peek had remembered, squirrels were chatterboxes. *This would be a good time for a stretch*, thought Peek. Maybe that would stop this squirrel from talking so much. She stood up on all four paws and arched her back into almost a "U" shape. Then she placed her two front paws way in front of herself with her claws showing, stretching out her back legs.

All the while, the little squirrel kept right on talking away. "I used to try to get in humans' houses looking for nuts, but it got a bit dangerous, so I stopped doing that, but I still run up to them and tap them on their shoes. They think it is cute and they give me nuts," he said. "What's your name? Did the humans give you a name? Do you have a family? Where's your family now?"

"So many questions from such a little animal," said Peek. "Yes, I have a name. It is Peek-A-Boo, and yes, the humans gave me that name. No, I don't have a home. I ran away from my home because the humans were going to give me away. I am sorry I intruded on you and your garden, but I needed a place to lie down, and this seemed like a good place to do that," said Peek.

"Well," said Cheeky, "the people who tend my garden have a porch, and you could probably stay under the porch if you wanted to. That way we could be friends and visit all the time! I would like that. Would you like that too? I know you are supposed to be my enemy and chase me, but for some reason, I'm just not afraid of you," said Cheeky, with a big toothy grin.

Peek, a bit surprised, looked at Cheeky and said, "I'm not your enemy; I'm not anyone's enemy."

"By the way," said Cheeky, "what do you eat? I hope you don't eat nuts, because I need as many as I can get for the winter."

Peek scratched herself and looked at the little squirrel. "Gosh you talk a lot, and very, very fast," said Peek.

She didn't mean to insult the squirrel, and the squirrel didn't appear to be insulted.

"Yup, yup, that's me, Chatty Cheeky," said the squirrel as he dug a hole and dropped a nut in it.

Peek was aware she was lonely and lost, and Chatty Cheeky was better than having no one to talk to at all. She followed the squirrel to the porch. Under the porch it was dark, damp, and cold, but the sunlight beamed directly on a chair on the porch. Peek jumped into the chair, circled around a few times, plopped down and promptly fell asleep. Cheeky left Peek alone to sleep and went back to his business of burying nuts.

Meanwhile, Peek-A-Boo's family returned from unloading some of the furniture and boxes at their new place. They looked for Cheyenne and Peek-A-Boo, because It was time to put them in their carriers and take them to their new home. Princess Cheyenne rubbed against their legs and her carrier, meowing to them that she wanted a cuddle. Mr. Smith picked her up and petted her, all the while looking for Peek-A-Boo.

"Well, Chy Chy, are you ready for the big move? I am sure you will love this new place, Princess. It has an fenced in porch for you to explore," said Mr. Smith.

The whole time he was speaking and petting Cheyenne, he was looking for Peek-A-Boo. "Goodness, Cheyenne, where do you think Peek-A-Boo went?" he asked. Now the man was getting very worried. He put the princess down and looked all over. He went upstairs and looked and then down again. He looked in all the remaining boxes, both full and empty. He went out on the deck and then looked around the outside of the house, thinking she had gone out an open door to avoid the bustle in the house. The man called her name repeatedly.

"Here, Peek-A-Boo! Here kitty, kitty, kitty!" But she didn't come.

When Mrs. Smith came back to the house, he told her he couldn't find Peek-A-Boo, and they searched together, but there was no Peek-A-Boo to be found. Mrs. Smith was upset and started to cry. She picked Cheyenne up and held her, all the while crying while searching. After an hour of searching inside and out, they realized that Peek was not in the house or on the grounds. They were devastated. The boys came back to the house and together they all went outside and searched, calling her name. They walked up and down their block, calling again and again for her, but Peek never came.

Mrs. Smith cried and cried saying over and over that she didn't understand why Peek would have run away. Mr. Smith could only hold his wife's hand and shake his head sadly. They left the house with more boxes to take to their new home, hoping that when they returned, she would be there.

Meanwhile, Cheyenne was beginning to understand what a terrible thing she had done. She couldn't tell the couple how nasty she had been, or that it was all her fault that Peek-A-Boo had run away. Cheyenne was miserable. When the couple returned to the house, they noticed how glum Cheyenne was and thought it was because she was so attached to Peek-A-Boo and missed her. They gave her lots of attention, the woman often crying while petting her. This kind of attention made Cheyenne even more miserable.

How can I enjoy myself, she thought, *when Peek might be in danger, hurt, or even worse?* She couldn't bring herself to think the worst, and she felt terrible for starting all of this in the first place. *Before, I just teased or made fun of Peek-A-Boo, but now, I really messed up,* she thought.

That night, Cheyenne slept fitfully. It was the worst night of her life. "What have I done? I don't even have any way to fix this. The family can never know, or they would take me to the pound and leave me . . ." she said aloud. Cheyenne swore she would never tell anyone what she had done and would try hard to make it up to the family for her lie. In the next few days, the family moved to the new house in the new neighborhood, never knowing what Cheyenne had done, or why Pee-A-boo chose to run away.

CHAPTER 8

THE NEW FAMILY

Peek awakened from a wonderful nap and stretched out as far as her body would go. The chair on the porch had been in the sun and she had felt safe, warm, and cozy when she fell asleep. Now she was hungry and knew she had to find a mouse or two for dinner. As she was about to jump down from the chair, she saw a car pull into the driveway and people get out. Although she was cautious, she waited to see if these people were going to be friendly or not.

"Pssssssttt, pssssssttt, get outta there quickly," said Cheeky. Before Peek could even move off the porch, a young girl came skipping around the backyard. The young girl spotted Peek-A-Boo and walked slowly toward her.

"Hello there, kitty," she said. She held out her hand for the big cat to smell, and Peek did just that. The young girl slowly sat on the porch steps and talked to the big cat. "My name is Megan, kitty, what is your name?"

Chatty Cheeky watching from a nearby tree was fearful for his new friend. He ran up to the little girl and tapped her on the foot hoping to distract her while Peek-A-Boo ran away, but Peek wasn't moving. Peek-A-Boo sensed that this was not a scary adult, but more like the boys in the Smith family. She rubbed against the girl's arm and began to purr. Megan, only distracted momentarily by the squirrel, gingerly began to pet Peek.

"I wish I knew your name, pretty kitty. I wish I could keep you, but I'll have to ask my grandmother," said Megan.

Peek sat beside Megan on the porch while Megan continued to pet her. Cheeky stood behind a tree and watched them. Half of him was afraid for Peek, and the other half was envious of all the attention Peek-A-Boo was getting. Cheeky ran up the tree and back down,

THE ADVENTURES OF PEEK-A-BOO AND PRINCESS CHEYENNE

trying to get Peek-A-Boo to look at him. He stood on his hind legs and waved his arms at Peek, but he knew he was being ignored. Just when Peek was getting comfortable with Megan, a voice inside the house frightened her, and she jumped.

"Megan, Megs, come in the house now, 'cause it's time for your supper!" Megan's grandmother shouted.

"Grams, come see who is outside on the porch. A kitty cat came to our house to be part of the family. Can I keep her, Grams, can I keep her, please?"

The grandmother came to the screen door on the porch and saw Peek with her granddaughter. She looked at Peek-A-Boo and saw she was well-groomed and that someone had taken good care of her. She knew that this cat surely belonged to someone and must have gotten lost.

"Well, Megs, I think that this cat might have gotten lost from her real home. I don't see any tags on her, so I guess we can keep her while we look for her real family, but you shouldn't get too attached because she belongs to someone else," said Grams. With that, she opened the screen door for her granddaughter and Peek-A-Boo, who trotted in after the little girl as if she had been living there forever.

The grandmother put out a saucer of milk and some dry cat food. She had purchased the cat food when she had owned a cat some years ago. Her cat had died, but she had never thrown out the food. Peek happily drank the milk and ate the dry food. She had become accustomed to eating dry and wet food at the Smith's house instead of catching mice, so this felt familiar.

Megan went upstairs and into her bedroom to do her homework and called Peek into her room. "Here kitty, kitty, come on up into my room with me!" said Megan.

Peek felt very safe in the house and with these people, so she marched upstairs into Megan's room to inspect it. She smelled the carpet, she smelled the desk, she then jumped on the bed and smelled the bed. Everything seemed to be warm and safe, so while Megan sat in the chair by her desk doing her homework, Peek curled up on her bed and promptly went to sleep.

Back at the old house, Peek's family was heartbroken. They had looked and looked for Peek-A-Boo and realized she'd run away. They could wait no longer as this was their final moving day, so they finished packing, just as the moving van arrived for their furniture. By the next day, the house was completely empty, and a sad family had moved to a smaller yet sadder home.

Cheyenne thought she could perk up Mr. and Mrs. Smith and the boys by being the cutest she could possibly be. She rolled on her back mewing like a kitten. She jumped in and out of empty boxes, playing hide and seek. She tried everything she could think of, but Mrs. Smith was still very sad.

What am I going to do? thought Cheyenne. *I made such a mess of things.* She knew she had to do something, but she had no clue where to begin.

A few days after their official move, the Smith boys placed posters with pictures of Peek-A-Boo everywhere. They waited, yet no one responded. Every day they went back to the old neighborhood and searched the area. They called the local pound to see if someone had turned Peek in. No one had. Eventually, they stopped going by the old house, and gave up ever seeing Peek-A-Boo again.

Peek, although missing her old family, and even Cheyenne, was content to live with this new family. The Smith's, although missing Peek-A-Boo a lot, had moved on with their lives. Only Chatty Cheeky and the Princess Cheyenne were not content with things the way they were. Cheeky wanted his new friend to come back outside to play, and Cheyenne wanted Peek-A-Boo back home so the family would be happy again.

CHAPTER 9

A PLOT TO RESCUE

In one of their long conversations while Peek was enjoying the sun, she had mentioned to Cheeky that she had lived with another cat, before she had run away. Cheeky was determined to find this other cat and help Peek find her original home. Chatty Cheeky traveled long distances, jumping from tree to tree, and had a large network of friends to help him. He had never been particularly brave, but he had a big heart, and everyone that knew him knew that about him. When he wasn't chattering, he was helping someone.

Since it was spring, most of the households had their doors open, and Cheeky could peer into their houses by hanging on the screen doors. It was the same as he had done years before. Cheeky started one block away from Megan's house and climbed on all the screen doors that were open, looking for a white cat.

Once, when Cheeky was holding onto the screen and peering in, a big dog ran over to the door and started barking.

"What are you doing on my screen door?" barked the dog. Cheeky was frozen with fear, but he managed to find his voice enough to ask if there was a white cat living there.

"No cat here," barked the dog. "But if you don't get off my screen door, there will be a dead squirrel on it!"

Cheeky jumped down and dug up a few plants on the porch, looking for nuts, before going on to the next house.

One day, one of Cheeky's cousins ran into him in someone's backyard, a few miles from where Peek-A-Boo was living. Cheeky was about to hang on the screen of this new house looking for the white cat, when Norbert, his cousin, ran up to him.

"Hello there Cheeky, how's it going with you? I heard you're looking for someone," said Norbert.

"Oh, hi, Norbert. Yes, I'm looking for a white cat that used to live with my friend," said Cheek.

"A new friend? Gosh, you're lucky, Cheek. You are always makin' new friends. Wish I could be like that. Is your new friend a squirrel like us? Is it a girl squirrel?" asked Norbert.

Cheeky shook his head. "You're always thinkin' about girls, Norbert. Girls, girls, girls!" said Cheeky. Then Cheeky described Peek-A-Boo in detail, all the way down to the white socks on Peek's feet. Norbert started to scratch his head. He rolled his eyes and looked up at the sky, and then down to the ground. He did this several times, as if he were trying to remember something, but couldn't quite remember.

Norbert and Cheeky's family were exceptionally large, with lots and lots of cousins and aunts and uncles. Norbert was one of the older cousins, and although he was one of the biggest squirrels around, all shiny black from head to foot, he just wasn't too bright. He was almost twice the size of Cheeky, but the family used to say that Norbert fell out of the nest, when he was younger, and he had changed. He seemed to be a little slower, not able to think fast or remember quickly after that. Cheeky, was the smartest of the whole family; small, and smart. He didn't care that everyone thought Norbert was slow, he loved Norbert, even though sometimes he frustrated him.

Cheeky tapped Norbert on the nose and said, "I'm talking here, Nort, pay attention, this is extremely important! What were you thinking about, anyway?" asked Cheeky.

Norbert scratched his head again and squeezed his eyes shut. Cheeky, a bit miffed, tapped him on the shoulder again. "Don't go to sleep when I am talking to you," said Cheeky.

"I'm not asleep, I'm just tryin' to remember where I saw a picture of the cat you were describin'," said Norbert.

"You saw a picture of Peek-A-Boo?" asked Cheeky. "Where, where did you see that picture?"

"If you hadn't distracted me by talking, I might have come up with it," said Norbert. "Let me think a minute . . . hhmmm . . . I think . . . No, that wasn't it," said Norbert.

By this time, Cheeky was excited and running in circles around Norbert, trying to get him to remember.

The faster Cheeky chattered, the more difficult it was for Norbert to remember. Finally, Norbert looked up with a big smile on his face.

"I remember now, Cheeky!" he said with great delight. Norbert was so proud of himself for remembering, that he almost forgot what he was remembering! "It was on a paper on a tree. I saw lots of pictures of your friend. The pictures were all over the trees," said Norbert, while still grinning about remembering that he had seen the pictures.

"Can you take me to these posters?" asked Cheeky.

"What are posters?" asked Norbert, never having heard the word poster before.

"The pictures you saw on the trees, Norbert, they are posters!" said Cheeky rolling his eyes and shaking his head.

"Cheek, follow me!" said Norbert. So, the two squirrels ran from the back yard to the front and down the street in search of all the posters of Peek-A-Boo.

The next morning, Megan and Peek found themselves curled up together in her bed. Peek stretched and yawned while Megan rubbed her belly. The sun shone through the curtains and the two seemed happy being together.

"It is Saturday today, kitty, and I don't have to go to school. We can play together all day. What do you think about that?" laughed Megan.

Peek didn't want to think about anything except how happy and safe she was here with Megan.

"Megs, come on down for breakfast!" called Megan's grandmother.

"Come on, kitty, let's go down and have something to eat," said Megs. Together, they marched down the steps and into the kitchen where Megan's gram was making pancakes. She placed a saucer of milk and some more dry food on the floor for Peek as well.

"Grams, I had the best night with kitty. We slept together all night. Can I please keep her? Can I?"

"That's 'may' I keep her, Megan," said her grandmother. "And you know very well we have to look for her real family. They might be missing her and sad. Suppose some boy or girl has lost their favorite pet? No, we have to ask all around the neighborhoods and call the pound to see if someone reported a lost cat." said grand-mother softly.

Megan was not happy, but she knew her grand-mother was right. "If I were that boy or girl, I never would have lost my cat," said Megan as she gobbled down her pancakes.

"Megs don't talk with your mouth full. After break-fast, we will figure out what to do," said Grams.

After breakfast, Megan and Peek-A-Boo went outside to enjoy the sun. Peek went to the back garden and to the bathroom while Megan played in the flowers. The sun was warm and being together made them both happy.

Five miles away, Cheeky and Norbert were staring at a poster that Norbert had chewed off a tree. The picture of the cat on the poster certainly looked like Peek-A-Boo and Cheeky was trying to figure out what the words on the poster said.

"Norbert," said Cheeky, "we have to take this poster to someone who can read humans' writing. Can you go and find Miranda for me? The poster is too large for me to carry, but I know she can pick up the poster and carry it," said Cheeky.

Before Cheeky was even finished with his sentence, Norbert was off looking for the little raccoon. Miranda was a small female raccoon that had been abandoned by her family. She had made friends with many of the animals around the neighborhood and gardens. Cheeky had watched her use her paws like human hands. He knew that she would be able to hold larger things than his little paws could possibly hold. Also, he liked Miranda a lot, but had never told anyone how he felt. He was very shy around girls.

Cheeky had heard a rumor that there was a fierce owl in the abandoned barn not far from where he had found the picture of Peek-A-Boo, and that some owls could read the human language. He himself was afraid of the owl because he knew owls often ate small animals like rats and squirrels, especially at night, but he would never admit to anyone he was afraid. He also heard that if the great horned owl liked you, he wouldn't eat you. Having listened to the gossip in the garden, Cheeky knew the great owl liked Miranda, at least enough not to eat her, and maybe enough to read the poster, and tell her what it said. Cheeky felt that this had become his quest in life (and maybe death), but he had to see it through for his new friend. He had wanted to follow Norbert to find Miranda, but he couldn't leave the poster on the ground by itself, and it was too big for him to take along.

So, Cheek sat down on the ground by the poster and waited for his cousin and Miranda to arrive. He thought about the danger he and his friends might encounter. He thought about what kinds of help his friends had given him in the past.

"I remember when it was sooo cold one winter, and I didn't have enough nuts to see me through. It was all the other squirrels that helped, so I didn't starve!" he said to himself. "I will not be afraid. I will do this!" he said boldly.

CHAPTER 10

CHEEKY & MIRANDA

"I will be back shortly," Megan said to Peek-A-Boo. "I have to go and see if we can find your family. I sure hope we can't find anyone who owned you, so I can keep you for ever and ever." She opened the door and let Peek in the house and shut the door once Peek was inside.

Peek waited a minute to see if Megan was coming in. When she hadn't followed the cat in, Peek ran up the steps, jumped on Megan's bed, and went to sleep. It had been over a week since Peek arrived at Megan's house and Grandma knew they had to look for her owners. Megan and Grandma went from house to house asking if anyone had lost a cat.

They started on one side of the road and when they were finished, they went to the other side. No one in their neighborhood had a missing cat. They went to the next block and the next and the next until they had covered several miles. Megan told her grandmother she was tired and wanted to go home and play with her new cat. So, Grams promised Megan that if they tried a few more blocks, they could go home.

One mile away from where Grams and Megan were searching, Norbert had found Miranda under someone's porch looking for grubs to eat. Norbert called her name and Miranda came out from under the porch. She was a small, beautifully round little raccoon, with a black mask around her eyes and white fur accents around the mask. Her little dark eyes sparkled when she talked or laughed, and she had long black eyelashes, which she batted when she was flirting. Her hands were black and human-like, and her feet were delicate with long black nails. Her light and dark fur seemed to shimmer with a silvery glow as she walked. When she spoke, her voice was soft and dreamy.

"Uh, ah, er, um," Norbert stammered in his very shy way. "I am Norbert," he said politely, "and I need you to come as quick as you can and talk to my cousin." The entire time that he spoke to Miranda, Norbert's face was as red as red could be, and he looked down at the ground making a circle in the dirt with his toe. Norbert told her that his cousin was on a mission of utmost importance, and that Cheeky was about to save the world. This greatly impressed Miranda, and she told Norbert she would love to help them save the world.

Off they ran to find Cheeky. All the while, Miranda thought to herself, *how wonderful it would be if a tiny animal like me could help save the world*. When the two got back to Cheeky, he was in the process of trying to fold the large poster of Peek-A-Boo and having little success.

"You must be Cheeky," said Miranda, smiling and batting her long eyelashes. *He is awfully cute*, she thought to herself. "I am Miranda the raccoon, and I am here to help you save the world."

Cheeky's head popped up quickly, and he looked from Norbert to Miranda and Miranda to Norbert. Cheek's eyes narrowed and he walked up to Norbert and bopped him on the arm, very frustrated with him.

"What did you say to Miranda?" he whispered, his face getting redder and redder. Norbert scratched his belly, hopping from foot to foot.

"Well, I kinda told her you were going to save the world, and you needed her to help . . . it's almost like savin' the world, isn't it?" asked Norbert.

Miranda realized very quickly that she wasn't going to be saving the world, and although she was disappointed, she was really getting a kick out of Cheeky's embarrassment. She crossed her arms over her chest, looked away, and pretended to be angry. Tapping her foot loudly, she twirled around and looked directly into Cheeky's eyes. She batted her eyelashes once more before speaking. "Exactly why do you want me here, Cheeky squirrel, and why did you tell Norbert to lie?"

Cheeky was so busy staring into her sweet, black-beaded eyes, and tiny button, black nose that he forgot to answer.

"Well, I am waiting for an answer," she said still tapping her foot.

Cheeky shook his head. It was as if for a moment he was hypnotized. His whole body froze, and his mind clouded up. He finally came out of his daze, shook his head, and found his tongue enough to say, "I am really sorry Norbert misled you, but I am just trying to help a friend, not save the world. My friend ran away from her home, and now she has been taken in by another human family. I am trying to read this poster, because I think it tells where she used to live. If I could read it, maybe I could get her back to her real home," said Cheeky.

Miranda listened to Cheeky, and her little heart melted. She understood how much he cared for his friend. "I think your wanting to help your friend get back home is a little like saving the world. You are certainly saving your friend's world, and that's really sweet," she said, smiling.

Cheeky's nose twitched, and he turned many shades of red, which is difficult to see, since his fur was black, and his scrawny tail bobbed up and down, up and down.

"What do you want me to do?" asked Miranda.

"I heard you are good friends with the great horned owl, and I need him to read this human poster for me," said Cheeky. "I can't carry it to him because it is too big for my paws, so I thought we could take it to him together and ask him what it says," replied Cheeky.

Miranda thought for a moment, chuckled, and then asked, "You aren't scared to go yourself, are you, Cheeky?"

"Heck, no!" said Cheek, puffing his little chest out as far as it would go and hoping she would believe him.

"Okay then, if you'll come with me, then I'll do it," said Miranda. With that, she took the poster in her little human-like hands, rolled it up, and started off down the road toward the burned-out barn where the great fierce horned owl lived.

The barn had been part of a farm many years ago, but the people had moved. The house was boarded up and the barn partly burned from a fire. Miranda knew that the old owl roosted way up in the rafters in the part of the barn that hadn't burned. So off they trotted; two scared but brave squirrels and one little lady raccoon, all in search of the great, fierce, and wise horned owl.

As this brave little group headed towards the barn, Megan and her grandmother were walking up the road towards the poles where the posters were hung. They

THE ADVENTURES OF PEEK-A-BOO AND PRINCESS CHEYENNE

had been searching and asking for days, going a little further each time; still with no luck. Megan was curious to see what the posters said, and she ran over to a tree that still had one hanging on it.

"Grandma, the cat on this poster looks like our kitty. I hope it isn't the same one, 'cause I really love our kitty and want to keep her," she said. The grandmother had caught up to Megan and was looking at the poster.

"Surely looks like the same cat to me honey, and the address on this poster isn't that far away. Maybe we ought to take a walk over to the address written on the poster and see what's what," said Grandma.

Taking the poster off the tree, the two walked further up the road toward the address written on the paper. Unfortunately, the poster had the old address on it, and not the new address where the Smith family had recently moved. The Smith boys had forgotten to put up different posters with the new address and their new phone number on it, but Grandma and Megan didn't know that, and they walked on.

Meanwhile, Cheeky, Norbert, and Miranda had almost arrived at the old barn, which was less than half a mile from where they had started. When they reached the barn, Norbert's whole body started to shake all over. His little black face was all sweaty, slightly pale, and he was weaving back and forth like he was going to faint.

Miranda turned, looked at Norbert, smiled, and gently said, "Norbert, it's okay, you can stay out here and stand guard for us. It's an important job and I know you'll do it well," said Miranda.

"Right, right," said Norbert. "I can do a very good job of standing guard waaayyy out here," he said with the color slowly returning to his face.

Miranda turned to Cheeky and looked at him. "Are you standing guard too, Cheeky squirrel, or are you coming in with me?"

"Me?" said Cheeky. "I'm coming with you. Whatever gave you the idea that I wasn't?" Miranda hid her smile as she headed into the barn to see the owl.

CHAPTER 11

THE TWO FAMILIES

The Smith family, who had originally adopted Peek-A-Boo, had settled into their new home. They had been busy unpacking, decorating, and planting plants around the house. During the daytime, they were too busy to think about Peek, but at nighttime, they often talked about where Peek-A-Boo could have gone, and how much they missed her. The eldest son was soon to start college and the youngest son was making friends at his new school. Both boys had talked a great deal about Peek-A-Boo running away, and knowing Cheyenne as they did, both believed she had something to do with Peek's disappearance.

The eldest son picked up Cheyenne, stroked her and asked her what she had done to Peek-A-Boo. Cheyenne would look as innocent as possible and purred as loud as she could, in hopes of distracting their conversation about Peek. All the while, the princess felt terrible about what she had done, and even though Cheyenne missed Peek-A-Boo, she would never ever let anyone know that she had lied to her friend. Her guilt seemed punishment enough for her. She really did feel awful about lying.

On that Saturday before the eldest son left for college, the two boys decided they would go back to the old house just for a bit of nostalgia and of course to see if Peek had returned. They knew the old house hadn't been sold yet, so they still had hopes of finding her. The youngest son couldn't get over the feeling that they would find Peek-A-Boo there, even though they had gone back time and time again. They made a plan that after their supper, they would ride their bikes down to the house one more time.

"I just can't shake this feeling that we are going to find her," the youngest boy said to his brother. The older boy shook his head but agreed to go one more time to humor his brother.

After dinner, they cleared the table and loaded the dishwasher before getting ready for their ride.

"Where are you guys going?" asked their mother.

"We're just taking a bike ride," the youngest said, shooting his brother a look that said, *don't say anything that will upset Mom again!* The youngest boy knew his mother had cried a lot about losing Peek, and he didn't want to upset her with false hopes again. It was about six o'clock that evening when the two boys took off for the old house. The boys biked slowly, talking as they went.

Megan and her grandmother had just arrived at the address on the poster and knocked at the front door. They waited and knocked again. No one seemed to answer, so they walked around the house and went to the back door. Megs noticed that there were no curtains at the windows in the back, so she peered in.

"Grams, there doesn't seem to be anyone living here. This room has no furniture." said Megan. Grams walked around the side of the house and looked in as well. Everywhere she was able to look, there was emptiness.

"Grandma, I don't think anyone's here anymore," Megan said again.

The grandmother looked at the poster and checked the address. This was absolutely the house that was listed on the poster. Grandma was baffled.

"Well, I guess that means we can keep her, can't we, Grams?"

Her grandmother sat on the edge of the porch in the back thinking a moment. This was certainly a mystery. Why would anyone take the time to make lots of posters and put the wrong address on it?

Megan was all excited. She wanted to go home right away and name her new kitty. "Come on, Grandma, let's go home so I can name my new cat!" she said with excitement.

Grandma didn't make a move. She was still thinking about the poster and hadn't heard Megan's request. Finally, Grams got to her feet and told Megan she was ready to go home. She guessed that someone had made a mistake on the poster, and it would be near impossible to find where Peek-A-Boo's family lived now. She took

Megan's hand and started to walk around the front of the house to head back home before it was dark.

Just as Megan and Grams were coming out of the gate of the empty house, they saw two boys biking toward them. The boys appeared to be exhausted. Grams saw that one boy was tall and thin with short blondish hair. He looked like the eldest of the two boys. The other boy was shorter, but not by much. He was slightly heavier with long brown hair pulled back in a ponytail. As they approached she noticed both boys had beautifully large round eyes and long lashes. The oldest Smith boy had very, light blue eyes, while the younger had beautiful hazel eyes that seemed to sparkle.

When Cheyenne was first given to the family, the oldest boy carried her all the time. She slept with him, played with him, and generally spent a good deal of time on either his or the youngest brother's bed. When Peek-A-Boo came into the family, after she overcame her shyness, she spent most of her time with the youngest brother, whom she loved dearly. Peek slept on the youngest's bed, sat on the floor by the shower until he finished, sat by him at the dining room table, and waited in the window for him until he got home from school. It was the youngest boy that Peek-A-Boo had missed the most.

CHAPTER 12

MATTATHIAS THE MAGNIFICENT

Miranda walked slowly and quietly into the barn, holding Cheeky's paw as tightly as she could without hurting him. When they were about halfway into the part of the barn that hadn't burned, she cleared her throat and called for the owl. "Mattathias!" she called out not very loudly.

"Wait, what's his name?" asked Cheeky. "His name is Mattathias the Magnificent. Matt-a-thi-us," said Miranda, spelling it as it sounded. "And he is the wisest animal for miles and miles around!" she whispered.

"Yeah, and also the fiercest night hunter of small animals such as myself," gulped Cheeky, moving closer and closer to Miranda. The little raccoon straightened her body to appear as tall as possible and called louder this time.

"Mattathias, are you here?"

Suddenly, a large, dark shadow swooped overhead, and came so close that the little squirrel could feel the wind from the wings across his cheeks. Cheeky shook uncontrollably, and his teeth began to chatter from fear. The huge owl landed on a rafter above the heads of Miranda and Cheeky and peered down at them. As Miranda and Cheeky looked above them, there was Mattathias standing two feet tall, with a wingspan of five feet. Cheeky couldn't stop looking at his eyes.

Female horned owls are larger, but Mattathias' family had unusually large males, and he was the largest. He was a terrifying looking owl with huge orange-yellow eyes and light orange discs (circles) around each eye.

"HOO-HOO-HOOOOOOOO-HOO-HOO!" shrieked Mattathias. His voice boomed and his beak snapped several times with a clack, clack, clack sound. Then, with a voice as strong as the wind that howls, the owl asked Miranda, "What are you doing in my barn little raccoon, and did you bring me that squirrel for my evening meal?"

Cheeky, who seemed frozen by the owl's eyes, started to sweat and thought he was going to faint. Miranda did not move except to hold Cheek's hand even tighter. Cheeky knew he had to appear brave, even if it was just for Miranda's sake.

"Oh great, wise and fierce Mattathias, I have come to ask a favor of you and your great knowledge," said Miranda. With that, the owl swooped down closer to a lower beam to see the little raccoon better. The owl's eyesight was not nearly as keen as his hearing.

"You are little brave, Miranda the raccoon, aren't you, the one who was abandoned in the field as a pup? I remember you. What do you want of me?" asked the owl. With that, the owl flew down to the lowest beam so that he was just above Cheeky and Miranda. It was then that Cheeky noticed the enormous talons on the owl and started to gently pull Miranda closer to the door opening. Miranda let go of Cheek's paw and stepped forward to address the mighty owl.

"I heard that you could read the writing of humans, and I have a big paper for you to read. It is most important that we find out what is written on it. It may save the life of one of our animal friends," she said. Miranda knew she was stretching the truth a little, but she felt that maybe if it sounded that important, and if the owl thought she was saving a life, maybe he wouldn't refuse to help her.

Mattathias peered at Miranda and Cheeky a long time. The silence in the barn was broken only by the pounding of Cheeky's heart. Then, Mattathias held out a claw with three large talons on it. Cheeky took the paper from Miranda, gathered up all his courage, stood as tall as he could, swallowed, and slowly walked forward toward the owl. His little feet felt as if they had lead weights in them, and his hands felt rubbery. He placed the poster in the talons of the owl and slowly and carefully backed away, never taking his eyes off the huge owl. In a flash, the gray and white horned owl spread his wings and flew to the top rafters with the paper in his talons.

"Wait here," he demanded as he flew to the top beam. "I shall read it and return to you shortly."

Having said that, Mattathias disappeared in the wooden beams at the very top of the barn, and Cheeky let out a very loud sigh.

"I heard that!" thundered Mattathias and made a deep throated sound that almost sounded like laughter.

Cheeky sat down quickly. His legs again felt like wobbly rubber and his throat was dry. Miranda stood very, very still and waited for Mattathias to finish reading the paper. All they heard was the rustling of paper from above.

"I hope he can help you," she quietly said to Cheeky, squeezing his hand. Then she became quiet. It seemed like an awfully long time before Mattathias returned with the paper in his talons. He laid the paper down in front of Miranda and looked her straight in the eye. "You know, little one, cats are not high on my list to rescue and save. Cats kill birds and owls if they can. Why would I want to save an animal that could harm some of my kind?" he asked.

"This cat is not a hunter. In fact, this cat is a friend of mine and she has never hunted any animal as far as I know," said Cheeky. Cheeky had stepped forward and was talking before he knew what he was doing. Of course, Cheeky never knew about Peek-A-Boo's past as a young cat, nor that Peek-A-Boo had hunted birds in her early years on the farm. "This cat ran away from home, and her family is missing her. She is a gentle cat and worth saving. Please wise Mattathias, please help my friend."

Miranda was looking at Cheeky and couldn't believe how brave he was. Mattathias was also looking at Cheeky, and Cheek thought he saw the beginnings of a smile on the great owl's face.

"What is your name, little squirrel? And how dare you address me when I haven't spoken to you!" boomed Mattathias in a voice that seemed to echo all around the old barn.

"My name is Cheeky the squirrel," said Cheeky in a shaky voice.

"Cheeky, you are either a very brave or a very stupid little squirrel. You knew I could have eaten you and still you came to ask my help. I think you are very loyal to your friends, and therefore, I will tell you where to find the house you are looking for," said the owl. With that, the wise owl began to read the directions to Miranda and Cheeky to help them find Peek-A-Boo's old house.

When he was finished reading, the great horned owl flew down a bit closer and peered at Cheeky. "Now that I have helped you, go away little squirrel, and do not come back again to disturb me, or the next time I might find that even your bravery cannot save you from being my dinner," he boomed.

The little raccoon and squirrel thanked the owl for his kindness and slowly backed toward the barn door, never taking their eyes off the old owl. As they went out the barn door, both thought they heard booming laughter from inside the barn. They looked at each other in disbelief. The two amazed animals accidentally knocked into Norbert, knocking him to the ground. Norbert was white as a sheet. He had peeked in the barn while still standing guard outside and had seen the huge owl. They picked up Norbert, who was still shaking, and ran as fast as they could toward the house where Peek-A-Boo used to live. While they were running towards the house, Cheeky and Miranda told Norbert everything that had happened inside the barn with Mattathias. Norbert's eyes were as big as saucers as he listened to their tale, stopping occasionally to shake his head or to whistle. Norbert whistled when he thought something was special. They ran and ran until they saw the house straight ahead of them.

CHAPTER 13

NEW FRIENDSHIPS

Just as Megan and her grandmother were opening the front gate to leave the house where Peek-A-Boo used to live, the two boys walked up to the house, holding their bikes. "Who are you and what are you doing here?" asked Megan.

"I could ask you the same question," said the older boy, "since this was our old house."

"We have been coming back here to see if we could find something we lost," said the youngest boy. Megan asked the youngest boy what it was that he had lost. "Our cat," he replied with a glum look on his face. "Our cat Peek-A-Boo ran away just before we moved, and we have come back many times looking for her, but haven't been able to find her," said the youngest boy.

Megan sat down on the ground and started to cry. "Oh, Grandmother, I knew I couldn't keep her, I just knew it! Why did we have to come here, anyway? Now our kitty will be gone forever," cried Megan. Then Megan cried even harder.

Her grandmother handed the poster to the boys and asked if this was their cat. Both boys were over-the-moon excited. They told her that they had put the posters up themselves, but no one had responded to them. The boys looked at the poster and realized they had the wrong address and phone number on it. Grams walked over to Megan, knelt, and put her arms around her.

"A cat that looks like the one on the poster showed up on our porch about a month ago, and we took her in," said Grams to the boys. Then she turned her gaze back to Megan. "I know you are sad, Megan, but isn't it better that we found our cat's real family? I am sure they missed their family pet a great deal," she said quietly.

The grandmother told the boys that she lived about five or so miles away, and they could bicycle to her home.

They should call their parents from her house to come get their boys, their bikes, and their cat. Grandma sat down next to Megan and hugged her for the longest time, until eventually she stopped crying. She and Megs stood up and started to walk toward their house.

"You know Megan, we don't live that far away," said the younger boy as they walked their bikes along. "So perhaps we would be willing to share Peek-A-Boo with you." Megs looked at the brothers and then at her grandmother. They all talked excitedly on their way back to Gram's house, and Megs was laughing by the time they arrived home. She ran in the door and bolted up the steps.

"Peek-A-Boo, Peek-A-Boo, here kitty kitty kitty! Come and see the surprise waiting downstairs for you!" called Megan.

Peek, who had been sleeping on Megan's bed waiting for her to come home, stretched, yawned, and jumped down off the bed, walking slowly towards Megan's voice. Megs found Peek-A-Boo in the hallway, picked her up, and hugged her.

"I have a big surprise for you, Peek-A-Boo, and I know you will be very happy," she said. She kissed Peek on the top of her head, gave her a little squeeze, and then carried her down the steps placing her down on the floor at the bottom of the stairs.

When Peek-A-Boo saw the Smith boys, especially the youngest boy, she was beside herself with happiness! She ran to the boys, rubbed against them, and weaved in and out of their legs. She meowed and purred until the youngest boy picked her up, held and hugged her. She didn't even mind he had picked her up from the floor instead of somewhere higher. Only then did she become quiet. The boys petted her for quite a while and then called their parents to tell them the great news.

When Mr. and Mrs. Smith arrived to pick up the boys, Grams invited them in for some pie. The two families immediately liked each other and had a wonderful time getting to know one another while they were eating. Mrs. Smith saw how much Megan adored Peek-A-Boo. Megan kept leaning down under the table and stroking Peek's tail, which Peek-A-Boo seemed to love.

Before dessert was over, Mr. and Mrs. Smith pulled aside the boys to have a conference. When they returned to the table, Mrs. Smith said, "Megan, what would you think about sharing Peek-A-Boo? Sometimes she could stay with you and your grandmother, and sometimes she would be at our home with the boys. What do you think about that?" she asked.

Megan couldn't believe her ears. "Oh, could we Grams? I would love that!" she squealed.

Grams nodded, and Megan jumped off her chair to give Mrs. Smith a big hug. Then she ran to Peek-A-Boo to give her a hug as well. Peek looked up at Mrs. Smith and began purring. Everyone seemed to be so happy.

Meanwhile, as the two families talked about their new plans, Cheeky and Norbert were hanging on the screen door listening to every word. Miranda stretched herself up on her back legs so she could see and hear what was going on as well. They were happy that Peek had found her original family, and glad she would be able to come back to Megan's house so they could continue to be friends. Cheeky and Norbert jumped off the screen door and sat on the back porch.

"Well, Norbert," asked Cheeky while gently patting Norbert on the back. Norbert was so happy, he jumped up and accidently fell off the porch.

"Well, Cheek," Norbert said dusting himself off from the fall. "I guess we saved the world after all, didn't we, Cheek? Huh, didn't we? Well, didn't we?"

"You bet, Norbert, we surely did," said Cheeky, winking at Miranda.

Miranda held Cheeky's hand, batted her long eye-lashes, and smiled her biggest smile, and then said, "You were very brave today Cheeky squirrel, and I am really glad I know you."

Cheek's heart started to thump, and he looked down to find that his foot was tapping as well. His tail twitched up and down, right and left, and he could feel his face getting hot.

"Why, I do believe that you are blushing. Are you, Cheeky?" asked Miranda.

"No, absolutely, positively not . . . well maybe a little bit," he said.

"Cheeky's got a girlfriend, Cheeky's got a girlfriend," sang Norbert, dancing around in a circle.

"Come on everyone, let's go back to the garden and get some food," said Miranda. "Then we can tell all our friends about the adventure we had." The three friends trotted back to the garden to eat, and to reflect on their day's adventures and share their stories with all their friends.

CHAPTER 14

A LESSON FOR THE PRINCESS

The Smith's arrived back at their home, put away their bikes and took Peek-A-Boo into the house. Upon entering, they noticed that Princess Cheyenne was nowhere to be found, which the family thought very odd.

"Here, Chy Chy. Come here kitty, kitty, kitty!" called the oldest son. Where are you?" the boys called, but Cheyenne was not about to come out.

She was sure that when Peek-A-Boo saw her, she would yell at her or even try to hurt her. She also knew that the family blamed her for Peek's disappearance, and that they would punish her for her lie.

As for Peek, she was so happy to be home, she ran from place to place smelling all the smells of the new house. She ran to the food bowls, jumped into all the new window-sills, ran upstairs, leaped on the youngest boy's bed, and snuggled down to have a nap. After looking for Cheyenne a bit more and knowing she was hiding somewhere in the house, the family turned out the light's downstairs, and went up the steps to get ready for bed.

Cheyenne, who had been hiding until everyone went to sleep, came out of her hiding place to get a drink of water and go to the bathroom. She did not hear Peek-A-Boo come up behind her as she drank the water.

"Hello, Princess, how are you?" asked Peek-A-Boo. Cheyenne whirled around until she was almost nose to nose with the one cat she didn't want to see.

"Uh, hello, Peek, how are you?" she responded softly.

"I am terrific, and it is great to be home again. I must say that I missed the family . . . even you, Princess," said Peek. Peek-A-Boo had decided long ago that if she ever made it back home again, she would punish Cheyenne, by not speaking about what Cheyenne had done to her. She figured that Cheyenne's guilt was a far worse punishment then anything Peek could ever say or do to her.

Cheyenne was flustered. She had felt terrible about the whole thing and wished she hadn't been so awful to Peek-A-Boo. She also knew she couldn't change what had happened. "Peek-A-Boo, this is extremely hard for me, but I have something to say to you, and if you interrupt me, I may never get it all out. So please don't interrupt!" said the princess.

"Okay, Princess, I won't," said Peek.

"First of all, please stop calling me Princess," said Cheyenne. "I don't feel very much like a princess, and I certainly didn't act like one. I am sorry for the whole mess I got you into. I lied to you about the family not wanting you, and it hurt them very much . . . and hurt you too. Mrs. Smith cried all the time you were gone.

I thought you were going to take all their love away, and I was jealous of you. I am sorry," said the little princess. Cheyenne had finished speaking. Her head hung down low and she couldn't look at Peek-A-Boo at all.

Peek felt sorry for little Cheyenne and waited a while trying to think of the exact words she wanted to say to the older cat. "Cheyenne, you are truly a princess. It takes a special kind of cat to look into their heart and admit they have done something harmful to someone else and to admit their mistakes," said Peek-A-Boo.

Cheyenne looked up at Peek with a strange, soft look in her eyes.

"When I arrived here at your home, Cheyenne, I was so scared that I didn't even think about how it would feel for you to have another cat here. I never thought you might be scared that the Smith family wouldn't love you anymore. I only thought about how scared I was, and how everything was so new. I am sorry you felt that way. I never want you to feel like that again. The Smiths love you very much . . . and I do, too!" said Peek quietly.

Cheyenne looked up from the ground and immediately went over to Peek-A-Boo and rubbed her head against Peek's chin. She rubbed against Peek so hard that she knocked her off her feet. Then Peek laid down on the bed and told Chy Chy to come lay down beside her to snuggle down for the night.

As the lights went out in the Smith household, the only sound you could hear was the loud purring that came from two incredibly happy cats.

9 781039 117938